FLESH of WHITE

I0727507

REMARQUE

ERICA J. HEFLIN

AMANDA RACHELS

Facebook: facebook.com/flatlinecomics
Twitter: @inversepress
Instagram: @flatline_comics
Substack: kevinlaporte.substack.com

FLESH OF WHITE presented by Inverse Press -
11101 Rachels Lane, Foley, AL, 36535.

ISBN: 978-1-938698-14-9

THE CREATORS

Erica J. Heflin & Amanda Rachels

Flesh of White was conceived in 2011 when Erica J. Heflin selected a Kickstarter reward securing the artistic services of Amanda Rachels for a 20-page story. By extraordinary coincidence, the two independently suggested a plot based on the plight of those with albinism in Tanzania. True story! The book in your hands is the culmination of their collaboration, but only one of several in total, including short stories and, certainly, more to come in future.

FLESH of WHITE

WRITER
ERICA J. HEFLIN

ARTIST
AMANDA RACHELS

COLORISTS
GAVIN MICHELLI
NATHAN LUETH
AMANDA RACHELS

There can be no limit to what we will do for our sons.

THERE IS A COST, AS IS TRUE OF ALL THINGS, MAJUTO. *
THERE IS NO COST THAT IS TOO GREAT.
* IN SWAHILI
YOU ARE THE HARVESTER, THE REAPER.
YOU WILL FETCH ME A GHOST.
THE BLOOD OF A GHOST, THE TEARS OF A GHOST, THE SCREAMS OF A CRYING BABE.
"THESE THINGS WE REQUIRE.
"GO NOW."

OUTDOOR MARKET IN TAMASHA, TANZANIA
HUSH NOW. EVERYTHING IS OKAY.
MAMA IS RIGHT HERE.

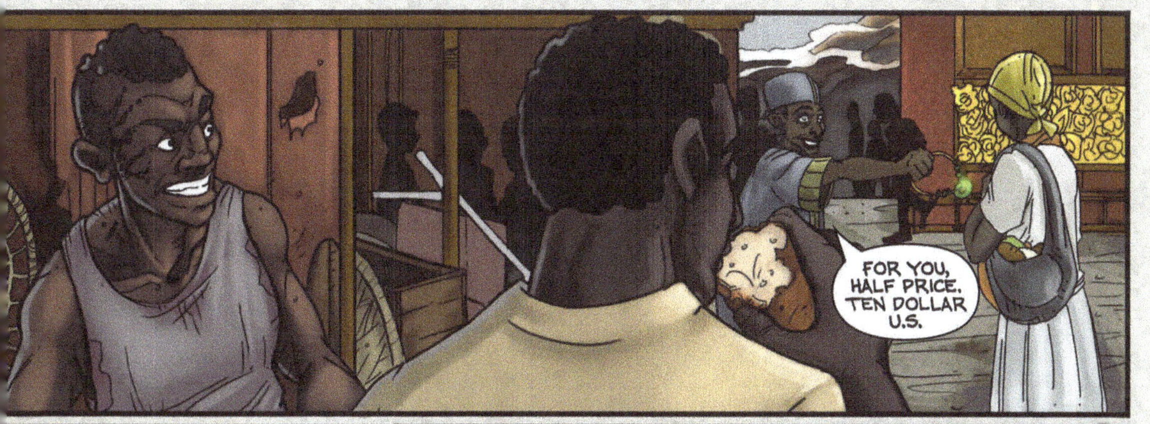

FOR YOU, HALF PRICE, TEN DOLLAR U.S.

YOU SOLD THE LAST FOR FIVE. YOUR WARES ARE NOT FINE ENOUGH FOR THAT PRICE.

WHAT'S THIS?

THE BABY--
IS BAD LUCK. LET US GO.

IT'S AN ALBINO.

BUT YOU ARE RIGHT. WE MUST GO. FORGET THE CHILD.

THE VILLAGE OF WASANDO

YOU'RE EARLY!

HE JUST SETTLED IN, LET HIM SLEEP. THE DAY WAS LONG.

WHAT IS WRONG? WHAT HAS HAPPENED?
ARE YOU HURT?

REHEMA, YOU WILL TELL ME?
YES, YES. LET ME GET KWASI SETTLED AND THEN I WILL EXPLAIN.

SLEEP NOW, LITTLE ONE. YOU ARE SAFE AT HOME.

THIS WASN'T ON OUR LIST.
BUT WAS NEEDED NONETHELESS. I MANAGED TO FIND EVERYTHING ELSE.

A COUPLE OF MEN IN TOWN SAW KWASI. THEY RECOGNIZED WHAT HE IS. HE NEEDED TO NURSE AND-

NO ONE WILL HARM OUR SON. I WILL PROTECT HIM.
UNTIL HE IS WEANED, I WILL MAKE ALL THE TREKS TO TOWN MYSELF.

NO ONE WILL HARM OUR SON.

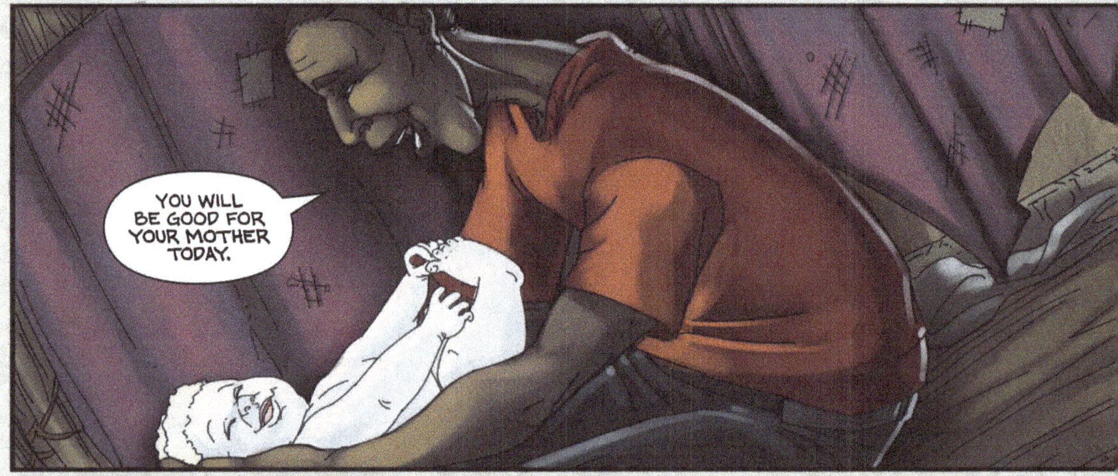
YOU WILL BE GOOD FOR YOUR MOTHER TODAY.

WOULD YOU WASH HIS SLING WHEN YOU GO OUT?
OF COURSE.

I WON'T BE TOO LATE TONIGHT, PROMISE.

MIND YOUR THOUGHTS. IDI AND HIS FAMILY ARE OUR FRIENDS.

AND WHAT OF MY FAMILY? MY SON? WE'VE BARELY THE HARVEST TO SUSTAIN US.

ANY MONEY GAINED BY THE BOY'S BLOOD IS MONEY THAT STAINS YOUR SOUL. DO NOT DISHONOR YOUR OWN FAMILY BY ENTERTAINING SUCH ATROCITIES.

HAS NO VALUE TO A PEOPLE WHO'VE SACRIFICED THEIR SOULS.

THIS IS KWASI'S HOME. HE WILL BE SAFE HERE. ANYONE WHO THREATENS HIS SAFETY WILL SUFFER THE CONSEQUENCES.

I WISH THE BOY NO HARM, BUT YOU KNOW AS WELL AS I THAT THE PRICE FOR HIS FLESH—

I WILL NOT FORGET THIS CONVERSATION.

I ONLY REQUIRE THE CHILD. PASS HIM TO ME AND YOU WILL LIVE.

WHO'RE YOU?

YOU WILL NEVER TOUCH MY SON.

AAAAAAH
UNGH!

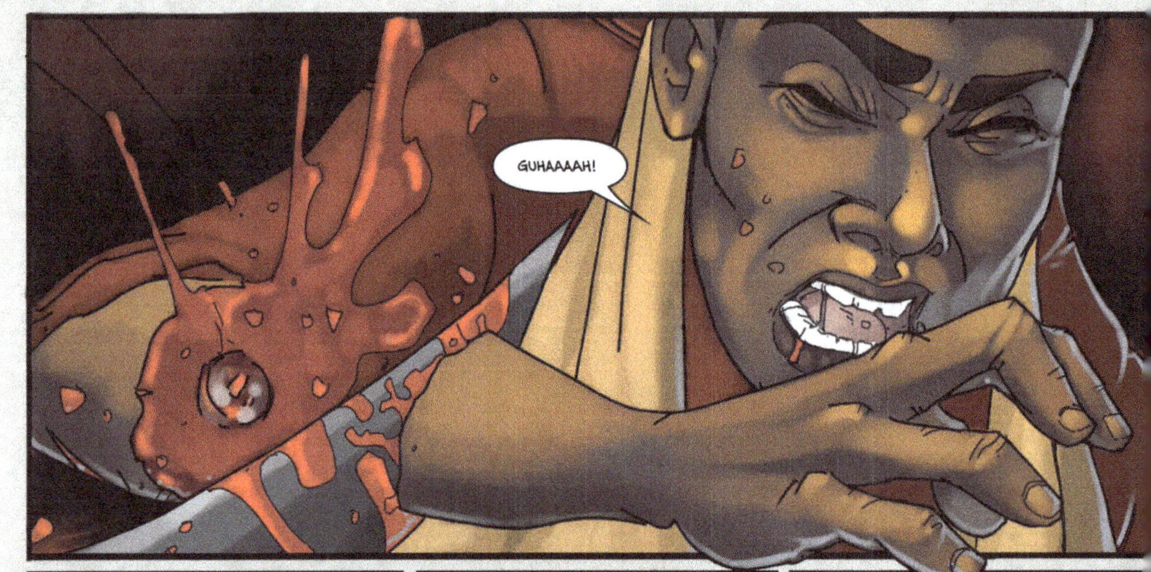

GUHAAAAH!

NEVER....
MY SON...

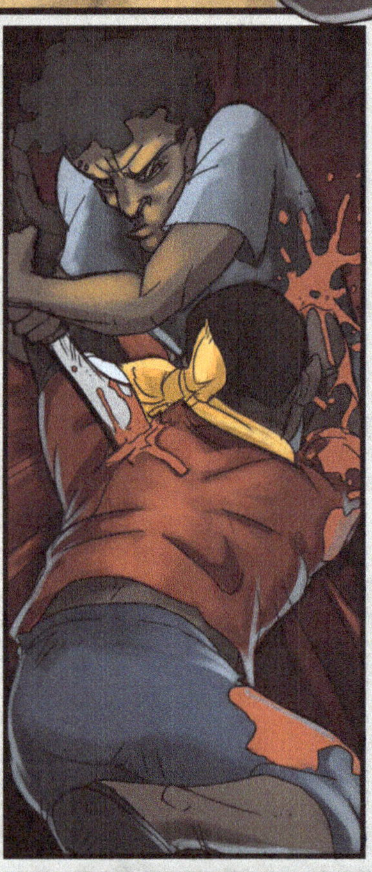

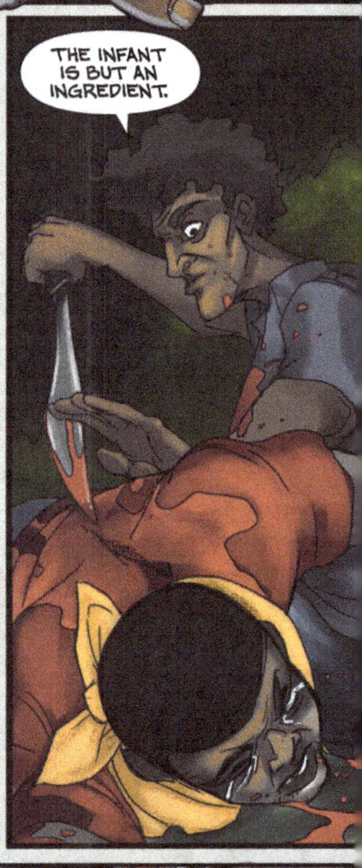

THE INFANT IS BUT AN INGREDIENT.

NOW YOU WILL DIE AND HE WILL MEET THE DOCTOR.

THE BABE?!

WHERE?!

I WILL FIND HIM.

YES, HE SCREAMED.

AS YOU WISH.

GO BACK TO THE VILLAGE.
FIND HAMISI, TELL HIM TO COME QUICKLY.
THEN YOU STAY THERE WITH YOUR SISTERS.

HAMISI! HAMISI! YOU MUST GO TO THE WATER!

CALM YOURSELF. SPEAK SLOWLY. WHAT IS AT THE WATER, CHILD?

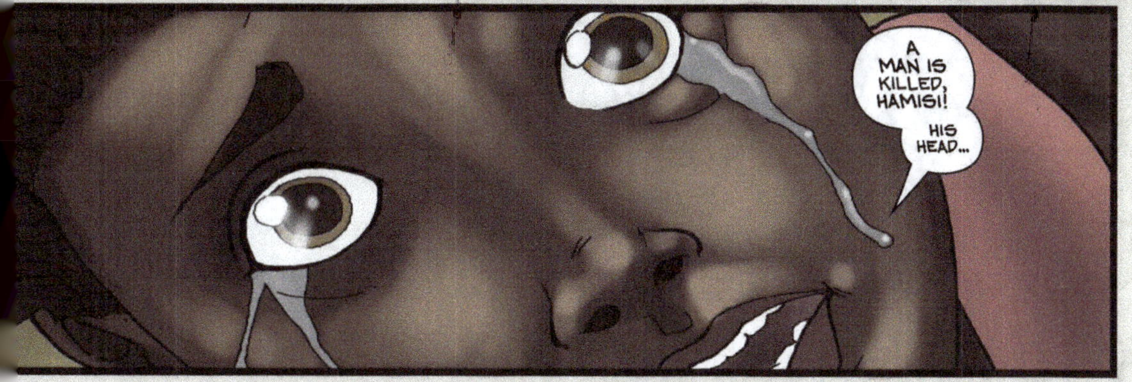

A MAN IS KILLED, HAMISI!
HIS HEAD...

I'VE SEEN NO OUTSIDERS.
THEN WHAT? YOU BELIEVE ONE OF US DID THIS?

YOU SHOULD ALL GO TO YOUR HOMES. REHEMA AND I MUST MAKE ARRANGEMENTS FOR IDI.

IT'S TRUE, ISN'T IT? THEY TOOK HIS HEAD AND HIS HANDS?
YES.

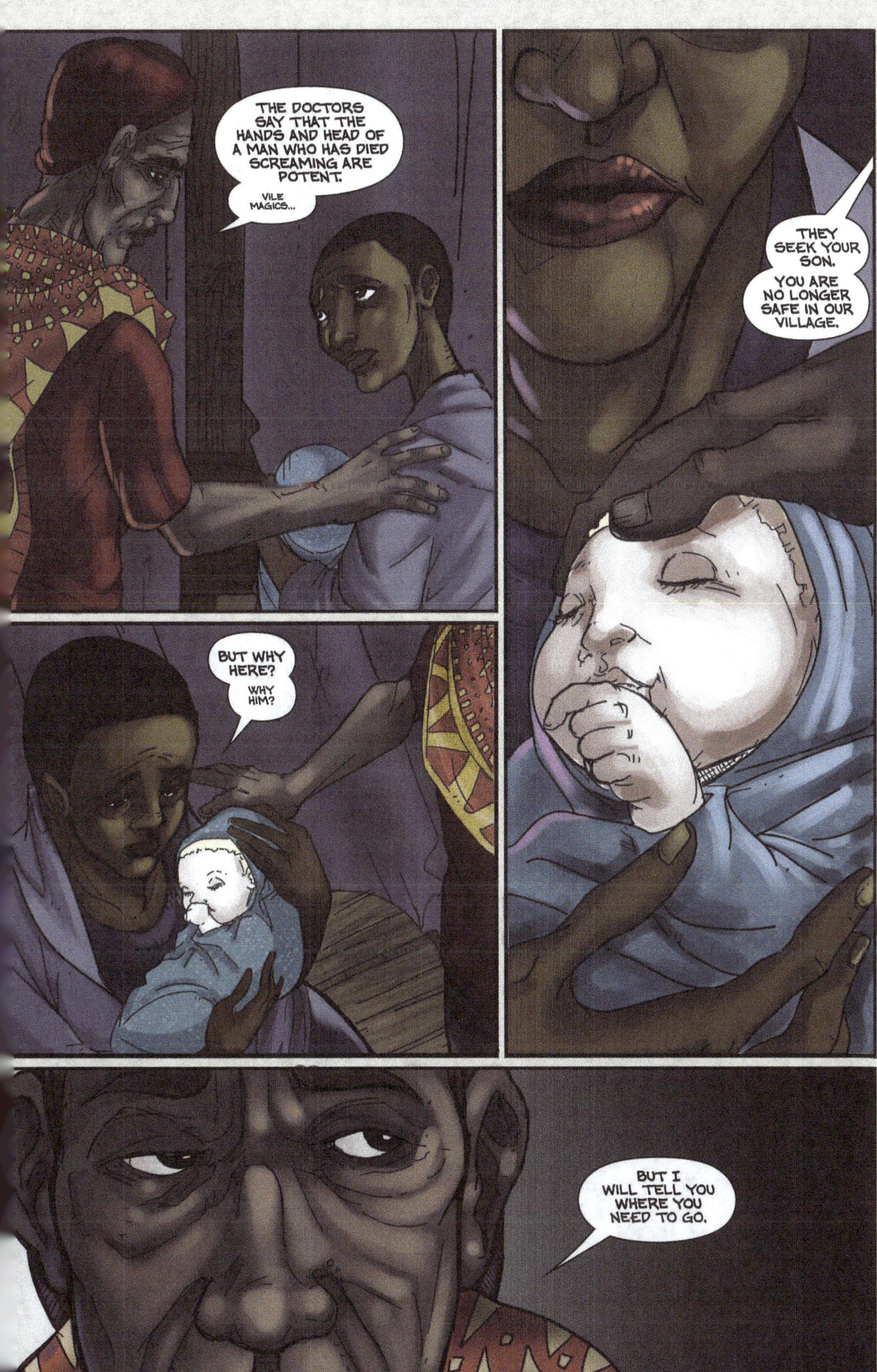

THE DOCTORS SAY THAT THE HANDS AND HEAD OF A MAN WHO HAS DIED SCREAMING ARE POTENT.
VILE MAGICS...
THEY SEEK YOUR SON.
YOU ARE NO LONGER SAFE IN OUR VILLAGE.
BUT WHY HERE?
WHY HIM?
BUT I WILL TELL YOU WHERE YOU NEED TO GO.

"THERE IS A CAVE THAT IS NOT FAR FROM HERE. I WOULD OFTEN VENTURE THERE AS A BOY.

"I DREAMED OF HUNTING. I DREAMED OF LIVING IN THE WILD. BUT NEVER DID I DREAM OF WHAT I WOULD FIND IN THAT DARK CORRDOR.

"IT WAS A THING MOST TERRIFYING. INHUMAN, I THOUGHT.

"IT SCRAPED ABOUT IN THE DARKNESS. I MEANT TO KILL IT. I WANTED TO TAKE THIS BEAST BACK HOME TO SHOW MY FATHER.

"HE DID NOT BELIEVE IN MONSTERS OR MAGIC. I MEANT TO PROVE HIM WRONG."

"BUT THEN I HEARD A NOISE I DID NOT EXPECT.
"I HEARD CRYING.

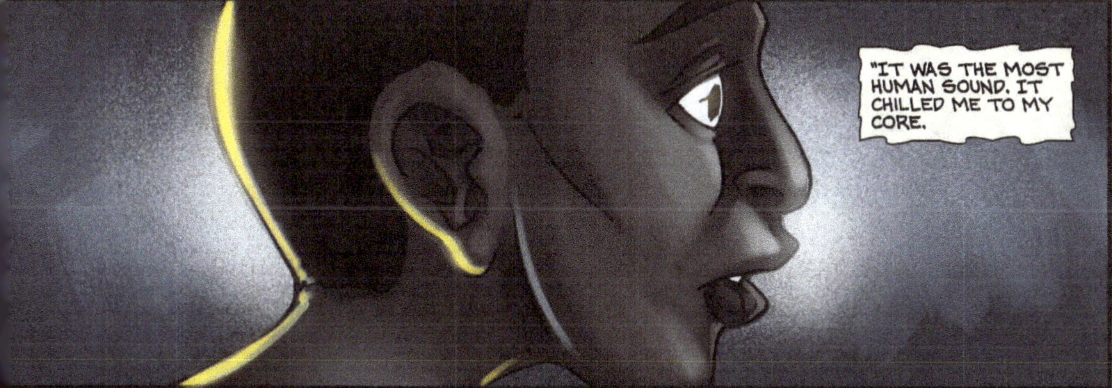

"IT WAS THE MOST HUMAN SOUND. IT CHILLED ME TO MY CORE.

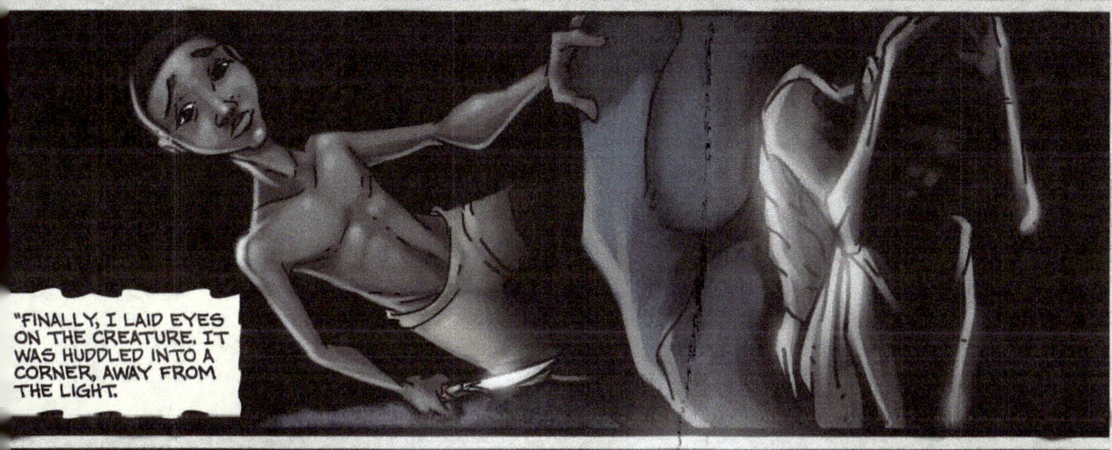

"FINALLY, I LAID EYES ON THE CREATURE. IT WAS HUDDLED INTO A CORNER, AWAY FROM THE LIGHT.

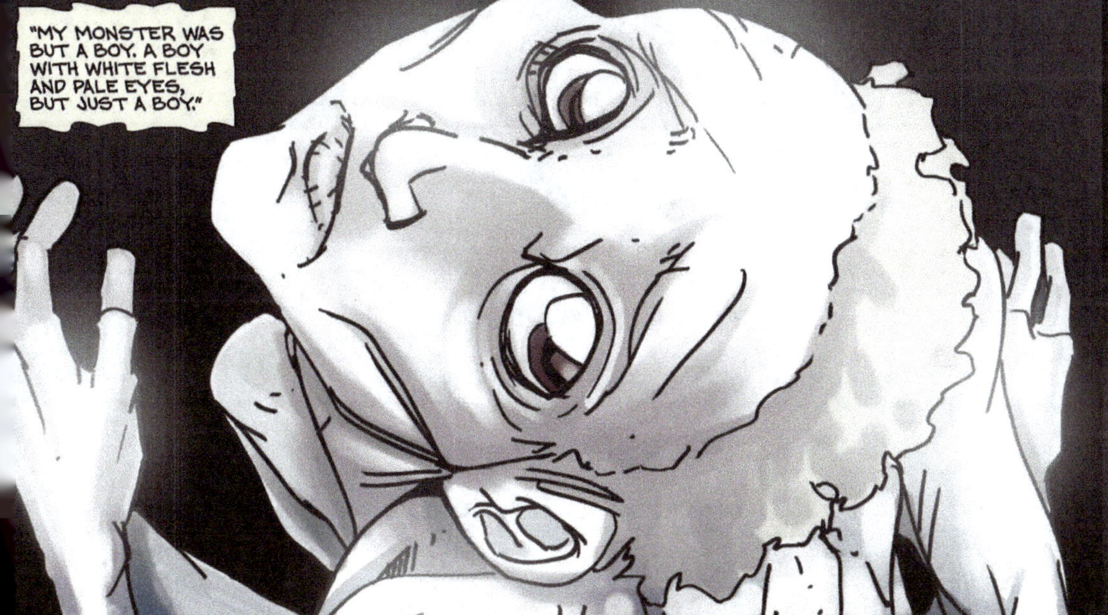

"MY MONSTER WAS BUT A BOY. A BOY WITH WHITE FLESH AND PALE EYES, BUT JUST A BOY."

"AT FIRST HE DID NOT SPEAK OUR TONGUE, BUT WAS EAGER TO PLEASE.

"HE BECAME ONE OF US.

"MY FATHER REMINDED ME THAT THERE WERE NO MONSTERS. THERE WAS NO MAGIC.

"BUT I STILL DID NOT BELIEVE HIM."

"THAT COWERING BOY BECAME MY BROTHER.

"IN THE NIGHT WE WHISPERED ABOUT OUR FUTURE.

"AND OUR PAST.

"WHERE ALL THINGS BEGIN.

"AND NOW WE HAVE COME FULL CIRCLE. YOU WILL TAKE YOUR SON AND GO TO YOUR FATHER'S FIRST HOME."

"THEY WILL TEACH YOU OF MONSTERS AND MAGIC.
"YOU WILL LEARN TO PROTECT YOUR SON.
"YOU WILL LEARN TO FIGHT BACK."
"THEY WILL TEACH

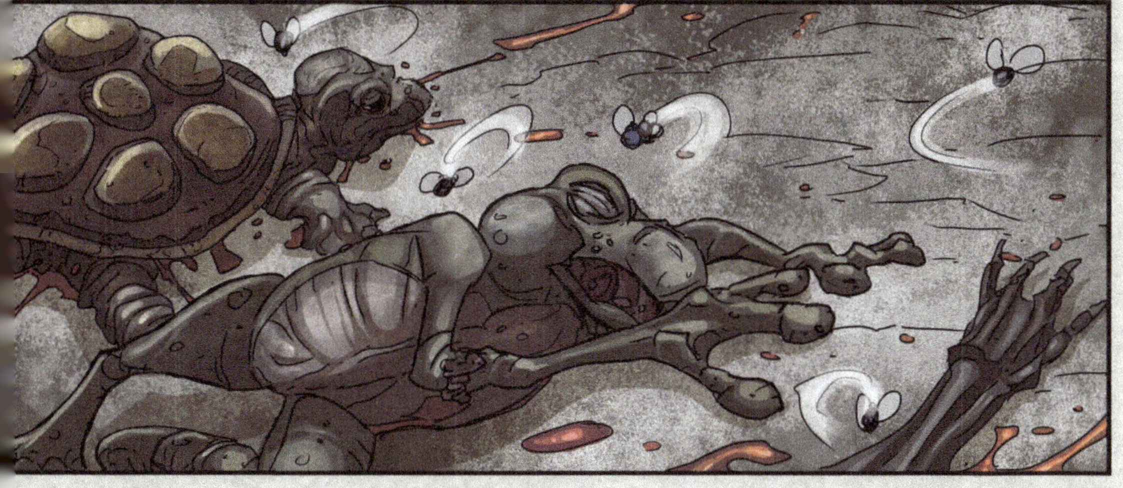

HE WILL
COME
SOON.*

* IN SWAHILI

BUT OUR PROTECTIONS-
STAY YOUR FEAR, MY FRIEND. HE WILL COME, BUT WE WILL BE READY.

WE... HA! IS SHE READY? CAN SHE PROTECT US? PROTECT KWASI?

SHE WILL BE. SHE IS OUR BROTHER'S DAUGHTER. HIS SPIRIT IS STRONG WITHIN HER.
BUT WILL THAT BE ENOUGH?

IT IS ALWAYS ENOUGH.

YOU FEAR THE DOCTOR'S CALL, BUT I EMBRACE IT. WE HAVE SPENT MANY YEARS HIDING FROM THE DEMONS OF THE WORLD. MANY YEARS... BUT IT IS OUR CALLING TO PROTECT THE NEXT GENERATIONS AS WELL.
THE DOCTOR HAS TAKEN TOO MANY OF US. KILLED INNOCENTS, COLLECTED THEIR SCREAMS AND THEIR FLESH.

WE GATHER TOGETHER FOR SAFETY, BUT WE MUST ALSO BE WILLING TO TAKE A STAND. REHEMA, BLOOD OF OUR BLOOD, IS A GREAT HOPE.
BUT YOUR MAGIC IS MORE POTENT! YOUR POWER MORE REFINED!

POWER IS BORN OF MANY FORMS. IF IT WERE NOT, WOULD MEN COME IN THE NIGHT, SEEKING OUR GHOST FLESH?
YOU MUST UNDERSTAND.

"SHE IS THE STRONGEST OF US ALL."

EXCELLENT! EXCELLENT. THERE IS MUCH JOY IN MY FUTURE, MAJUTO. MUCH JOY!

THE COST IS UNFORTUNATE, OF COURSE, BUT THAT IS A LUXURY OF MARRIAGE AND BIRTH, NO?

NOT A SORE POINT, I HOPE.

NOT AT ALL.

THIS IS FOR BAKARI?

COME, HARVESTER. SHARE THE FRUITS OF YOUR LABOR.

PERHAPS. HE ASKS FOR A SPELL OF LOVE, BUT DESIRES A SPELL OF OWNERSHIP. WHICH DO YOU THINK I SHOULD GIVE?

OR WOULD YOU RATHER I GIVE HIM NONE? HMM?

I CARE NOTHING FOR THE WEASEL. I JUST WANT MY SPELL COMPLETED. AND THEN I WILL LEAVE YOU.

AND THEN YOU WILL NEVER LEAVE ME! BUT IT IS NOT I WHO FAILED. IT IS NOT I WHO HAS LOST THE ONLY THING THAT MATTERS...

HAVE NO WORRY. YOUR DOCTOR SEEKS ONLY TO ASSIST. CLOSER NOW. THE FINAL PATHWAY. THE FINAL DOOR.

"GIVE ME HIS EYES, THAT I MAY SEE."

YES, THESE WILL SUFFICE.

I BELIEVE THEY'RE THE SAME COLOR,

WOULD YOU LIKE TO KNOW WHAT HAPPENED TO HIS ORIGINALS, HMM?

NO? WELL THEN, HARVESTER, FETCH A SNAKE OF APPROPRIATE GIRTH.

COME NOW, IDI, GHOST FATHER OF GHOST SON.

"GUIDE US."

"SEEK THE FLESH OF YOUR FLESH."

"LOVE OF YOUR LOVE."

"FURTHER.!"

"UGKK. OBEY, SERVANT."

"WE NEED ONLY TO GET OUR BEARINGS. AND THEN, AGAIN, YOU WILL HARVEST."

I FEEL VERY FORTUNATE TO HAVE THIS PLACE... LIFE BEFORE... IT WAS VERY DIFFICULT.
MY FATHER SPOKE LITTLE OF HIS TIME HERE... OF ANY TIME BEFORE HE CAME TO US, BUT I BELIEVE THAT HE LOVED IT HERE.

I'M SURE HE DID, BUT A WANDERING SPIRIT CANNOT BE CONTAINED. HE WAS FORTUNATE TO END UP WHERE HE DID, AND MEET THOSE WHO WOULD COME TO LOVE HIM.

I WAS ONE OF SIX CHILDREN, AND THE ONLY ONE WITH ALBINISM. MY MOTHER AND FATHER LOVED ME A GREAT DEAL, BUT ULTIMATELY THEY COULD NOT PROTECT ME FROM THOSE WHO WOULD SEEK TO DO ME HARM.

WHEN I CAME HERE, PREGNANT AND ALONE, DEATH SEEMED A CERTAINTY... BUT WE HAVE ACCESS TO MEDICINES, AND THE WORLD HERE IS QUIET AND WELCOMING.
MY PRESENCE... IT'S CHANGED THAT, HASN'T IT?

YES, BUT YOU ARE NOT TO BLAME FOR THE ACTIONS OF OTHERS. THERE IS A WAR BEING WAGED...
WE BATTLE IGNORANCE. WE BATTLE EVIL... IT WAS BOUND TO FIND ITS WAY TO OUR BORDERS EVENTUALLY. ALL WARS DO.

THE DAY-TO-DAY CONCERNS OF OUR LIFE HERE WEIGH MORE HEAVILY ON ME. WILL I LIVE TO SEE THE MAN THAT MY SON BECOMES?
I SHARE THOSE SAME FEARS... AND I FEAR FOR KWASI. HIS FATHER... GONE. MY FATHER ALSO LEFT US WHEN HE WAS YOUNG...

CANCER?
IT IS ALL TOO COMMON, BUT WITH EACH GENERATION WE GAIN MORE WISDOM AND BETTER HEALTH. LIFE FOR YOUR SON WILL BE BETTER THAN IT WAS FOR YOUR FATHER.

HAVE YOU BEEN DIAGNOSED?
WITH CANCER? NO. BUT WHERE I AM FROM, MANY BELIEVE THAT BEDDING AN ALBINO WOMAN CAN CURE THEM OF DISEASE. OF AIDS.

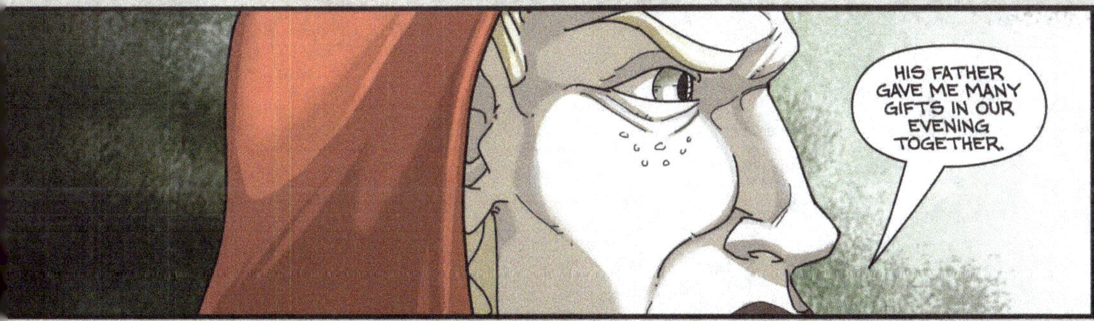

HIS FATHER GAVE ME MANY GIFTS IN OUR EVENING TOGETHER.

I'M SORRY...
I AM BLESSED THAT I RECEIVE TREATMENT, AND THAT MY SON HAS AVOIDED THAT FATE.

I PROMISED THEN, AS I PROMISE NOW, THAT OUR SONS WILL BE BETTER MEN THAN THE BEST WE'VE KNOWN. THAT IS OUR OBLIGATION.

"FEEL THEM.

"AH, YES. CLOSER STILL. TAKE US TO THE PATH, IDI.

"THE PATH, THE CITY, THE SUN TO THE EAST. YES, AT LAST! I KNOW FROM WHENCE SHE CAME.

"I KNOW WHERE SHE TRAVELS!"

ERAGH!

NO MATTER, NO MATTER, I HAVE WHAT WE NEED.

FETCH MY THINGS, HARVESTER. I WILL NOT ALLOW YOU TO FAIL AGAIN.
I AM YOURS TO COMMAND, DOCTOR.

AH, PLEASE, TAKE YOUR SEAT, REHEMA.
ARE YOU WELL THIS DAY?
I AM WELL, WILLIAM.

I AM PLEASED TO HEAR IT. KWASI GROWS. YOU GROW. THIS IS AS IT SHOULD BE.
DO YOU HEAR THAT? THE BIRDS HAVE RETURNED...

WE, AS MAGICIANS OF THE NATURAL ORDER, TAKE OUR CUES FROM THE WORLD AROUND US. WHEN THE BIRDS ARE SILENT, WE SHOULD LISTEN FOR WHAT COMES... WHEN THEY SING, WE MAY JOIN THEM IN SONG.
BUT I AM NO MAGICIAN, NO WITCH. I HAVE COME TO YOU DAY AFTER DAY, MONTH AFTER MONTH, AND YOU TEACH ME TO SIT... AND TO BREATHE.

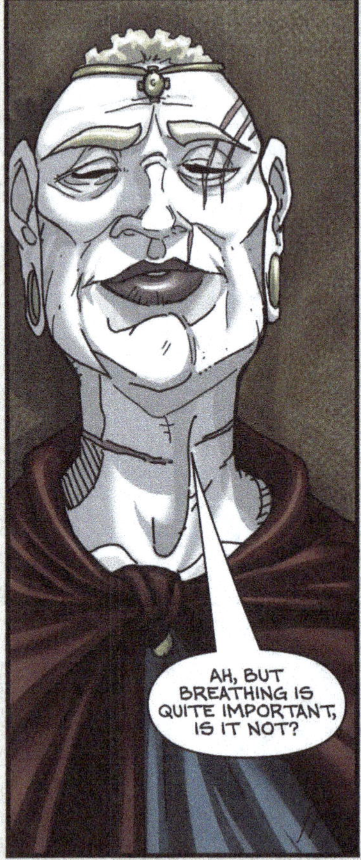

AH, BUT BREATHING IS QUITE IMPORTANT, IS IT NOT?

I TEACH YOU SERENITY. WE HEAR BETTER, LEARN MORE, WHEN OUR HEARTS AND MINDS ARE STILL. WITH EACH DAY HERE YOU LEARN OF THE EARTH, AND SHE WHO IS THE SOURCE OF ALL OUR MAGIC. SHE IS LESS DIRECT, LESS OVERT THAN THE KEEPER OF THE BLOOD, BUT HER POWER LINGERS, WHERE HIS FADES.

YOU LEARN MORE THAN YOU KNOW.

YOU HAVE YOUR FATHER'S SPIRIT, REHEMA. YOU WILL HAVE TO CALL UPON IT IN THE DAYS TO COME, AND CARRY FORWARD WITH NO REMORSE AND NO ANGER. THE POWER THAT GUIDES YOU MUST COME FROM YOUR LOVE FOR YOUR SON.
TO MOVE FORWARD, YOU MUST LET GO OF PAIN.

IDI...

THE WAY HE WAS TAKEN FROM ME... THE WAY HIS BODY WAS LEFT BEHIND...
HE WAS A MAN! AND HE WAS DISCARDED!

HOW CAN I NOT HATE THEM?

WE ARE EMOTIONAL CREATURES. THAT YOU HATE THEM FOR WHAT THEY HAVE DONE AND WHAT THEY TOOK FROM YOU IS AS IT SHOULD BE. BUT TO HEAL, TO MOVE FORWARD, AND TO SAVE YOUR SON, YOU WILL MOVE PAST IT.
YOU WILL DO SO BECAUSE THAT IS THE ONLY WAY.

IDI?!

AH, YES... AT LAST HE COMES.
THIS IS ALL THAT REMAINS OF YOUR HUSBAND IN THIS WORLD. THIS IS HIS LOVE FOR YOU AND HIS LOVE FOR KWASI.

HE'S COME TO SAY GOOD-BYE?

YES. HE MUST JOIN WITH HIS SELF THAT IS IN THE WORLD BEYOND. IT IS LONG PAST HIS TIME.

THERE COMES THE STILLNESS WITHIN.
BLESSED ARE WE WHO ARE LEFT BEHIND. BLESSED ARE THEY WHO PASS BEYOND THE VEIL.

BUT WHY WOULD HE STILL BE HERE, AFTER ALL THIS TIME? CAN LOVE BIND THE SPIRIT?

LOVE... SELF-SACRIFICE, THESE THINGS ARE BINDING. THEY CREATE THE WEB OF LIFE, THE UNSEEN THREADS THAT CONNECT US ALL TO ONE ANOTHER. THEY ALLOW OUR SPIRITS TO PROTECT THOSE WE LOVE LONG AFTER WE'VE MOVED ON.
ARE YOU SAYING IDI HAS BEEN WITH US, WATCHING OVER US, ALL THIS TIME?
NO... I FEAR THAT HIS LINGERING SPIRIT WAS NOT OF HIS VOLITION.

STILL YOUR HEART. HE IS IN A PLACE OF NO PAIN OR SORROW NOW. WHAT LED HIM THERE CAN DO HIM NO HARM.
THOUGH KWASI WAS NOT CRADLED IN HIS ARMS, HE DIED FOR HIM. FOR US, THAT IS BEAUTY AND IS POWER, BUT FOR OUR ENEMIES IT IS DANGER.

THEN THEY CAN'T HURT HIM ANYMORE?
NEVER AGAIN. HE IS AT PEACE.

AND SO THEY DESECRATED HIS BODY? AND... AND THEY TOOK HIS HEAD.
YES, FOR THAT REASON, AND OTHERS. BUT HIS SPIRIT IS NO LONGER TIED TO THEM.

YOUR QUESTION... SAY IT ALOUD.
I... THIS PLACE, THESE THINGS... THEY HAVE NO SMELL.

AH. YOUR MIND HAS NOT YET ENTIRELY FAILED YOU, IT SEEMS.

THE SCENT OF CARRION SUMMONS THE FLIES, SUMMONS THE SICK-MAN, SUMMONS THE SPIRITS OF THE GATEWAY BETWEEN LIFE AND DEATH.
MEN ARE NOT MEANT TO FACE THEM UNTIL THE MOMENT IN BETWEEN. TO DO SO... ONLY FOOLS WOULD DO SO.

I AM NO FOOL.

THIS IS NOT... NOT ALL... MY-

TAH! HE IS NOT HERE.

I PRESERVE HIS FLESH WITH THE INGREDIENTS YOU BRING TO ME. HIS BRAIN WILL NOT ROT AWAY. HIS HEART WILL NOT WITHER.

I WILL RETURN HIM TO YOU... INTACT.

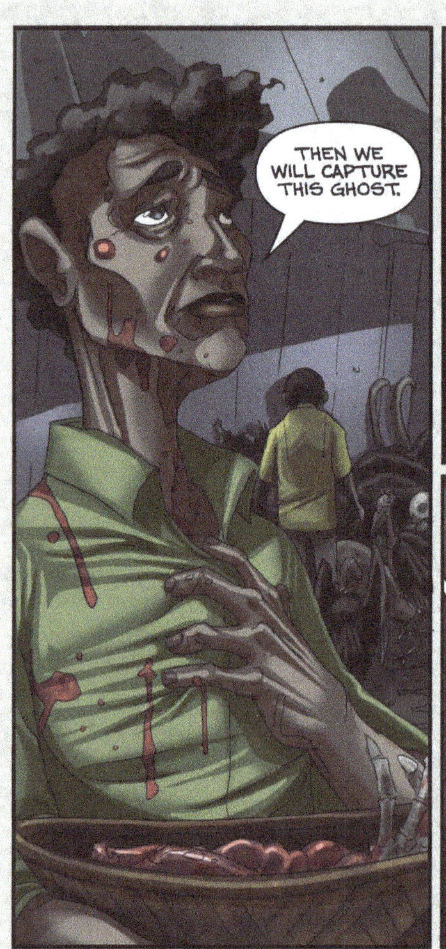

THEN WE WILL CAPTURE THIS GHOST.

IT SUCKLES STILL FROM THE MOTHER'S BREAST.

THE BOND IS STRONG. THE POWER OF THE FLESH IS STRONG.

YOU WILL BE TASKED WITH STIFLING ITS SCREAMS. YOUR BOND TO YOUR SON WILL OVERPOWER THEIR BOND, ALLOWING MY MAGIC TO WORK.

AS YOU COLLECT THE GHOST, I WILL TEND TO THE OTHERS.

MANY WILL DIE. THOSE OF WHITE FLESH, POWER POTENT, WILL FALL TO THE EARTH. I WILL GATHER THEIR SCREAMS AND TAKE THEIR HEADS.
I WILL HAVE USE FOR THEM ALL.

BUT THEY'LL HAVE THEIR OWN SORCERY, MAGICS, AND BARRIERS.
AND I WILL TEND TO THEM! THEIR ABILITY IS NOTHING BUT A MEANS OF DELAY.

I WILL MAKE THE PATH CLEAR FOR YOU. YOU NEED ONLY TAKE THE BABE IN YOUR ARMS--

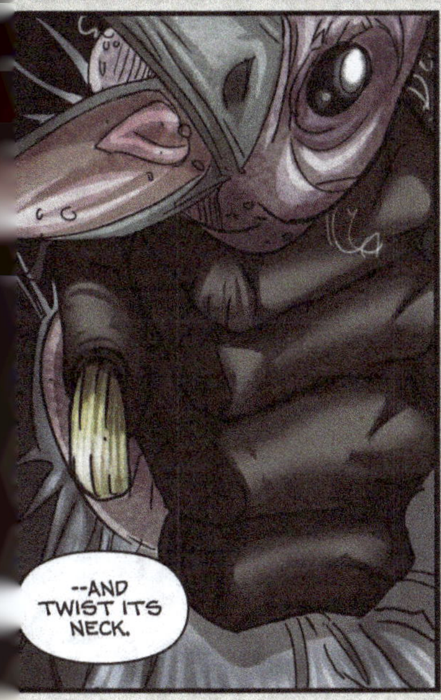

--AND TWIST ITS NECK.

FEEL ITS HEART BEAT, SLOWLY, SLOWLY, UNTIL IT BEATS NO MORE.

IT'S MORNING...
A NEW DAY.

WE SAID THAT WE WOULD TEACH YOU TO PROTECT YOUR SON, AND WE ARE...
BUT YOU CANNOT DEFEAT THE DOCTOR'S MAGICS. NONE OF US COULD, EVEN IF WE STOOD TOGETHER. YOU UNDERSTAND?
YES.

YOU'RE TEACHING ME HOW TO DIE, SO THAT HE MAY LIVE.

YESTERDAY

THE TIME IS UPON US THEN...

HE COMES.

NOW.
I'M SURPRISED TO FIND YOU HERE.
YOU'VE HEARD WHAT NASREEN ENCOUNTERED? THE SERPENT SPY?

I HAVE. THE DOCTOR WILL BE COMING SOON... COMING FOR US ALL.
YES! AND YET STILL YOU SIT. OUR BROTHERS ARE PREPARING FOR WAR.

KNOW THIS, SHAMIRA. IF A KNIFE IN MY HAND WOULD SAVE MY SON, I WOULD KILL. BUT I HAVE BEEN GIVEN SOMETHING ELSE, THE INTANGIBLE STRENGTH OF EMOTION.

THE BEAST THAT HUNTS ME, THAT HUNTS MY SON, DRAWS EVER NEARER AND THIS IS ALL I CAN DO. IT IS WHAT I MUST DO.
I WILL FOREVER CARRY THE MEMORY OF MY HUSBAND'S CORPSE, BUT SO TOO DO I CARRY HIS LOVE.

KWASI CARRIES OUR LOVE. IT IS OUR STRENGTH.

LET THE MEN GATHER THEIR ARMS. THEY WILL BE NEEDED.

WHAT OF YOU, MY FRIEND? HOW WILL YOU DO BATTLE WHEN THE MOMENT COMES?

I... I HADN'T...

I WILL TEND TO THE YOUNG CHILDREN WHO CANNOT STAND AGAINST THE COMING RAGE. I WILL KEEP THEM HIDDEN. I WILL BE THE LAST LINE.

THERE CAN BE NO LIMIT TO WHAT WE WILL DO FOR OUR SONS.

ARUSHA, TANZANIA. THREE YEARS AGO.
YOU WILL QUIET YOUR-SELF, OR I WILL QUIET YOU!
I WILL SAY WHATEVER I WISH.

THOUGH YOU CAN TRY TO STOP ME IF YOU LIKE.

HMH.

GUYS, STOP IT!

LET IT GO!

AH! ENOUGH, ALRIGHT?

I'VE MISSED DINNER. I'M SORRY...
YAHMI, WHAT'S HAPPENED? WERE YOU ATTACKED?
NOTHING LIKE THAT, BABA. JUST AN ACCIDENT.
I SEE...
WILL I NEED TO GO TO THE HOSPITAL?
NO, SON, NO HOSPITAL. I'LL CLEAN IT OUT AND STITCH IT UP, BUT YOU MUST USE MORE CAUTION!

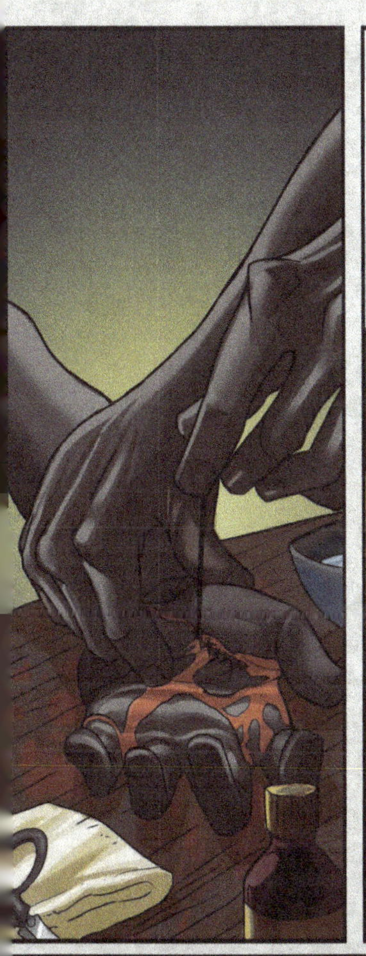

BABA!

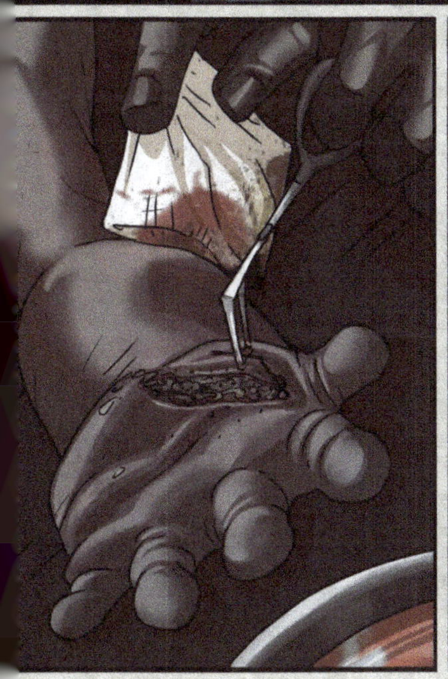

WELL?!

WHAT DID SHE SAY? WHAT WILL SHE DO?

SHE IS PREPARING AS BEST SHE CAN.
SHE BROUGHT THE HUNTER TO OUR HOMES!

AND NOW SHE CURLS UP TO DIE AS PREY?
HER BATTLE IS NOT ONE THAT YOU AND I CAN UNDERSTAND, MY FRIEND. THE NATURE OF THEIR WAR IS OF THE SPIRIT.

SO NOW YOU SPEW THE SAME RHETORIC AS WILLIAM? MEANINGLESS WORDS WITH NO POWER?
SHE IS BRINGING US DEATH.

YES. DEATH. IN THE COMING DAYS I MAY BURY MY SON. OR THERE MAY BE NONE TO BURY ME...

BUT EVERY TIME I SIT AT HER SIDE, I KNOW THAT THIS IS THE PATH THAT WE MUST TREAD. THE DOCTOR'S POWER IS TIED TO THE BOY - TO THE PURE FLESH OF WHITE.
AS I SWALLOW THE FEAR THAT MY SON MAY BE KILLED IN THE COMING BATTLE, I ACCEPT THAT IF KWASI IS TO FALL ALL THE HOPES AND DREAMS FOR THIS VILLAGE - OF MY HEART - WILL BE DROWNED IN BLOOD AND BURIED IN A SHALLOW GRAVE.

REHEMA GIVES ME STRENGTH. KWASI GIVES ME HOPE. WE WILL ALL PLAY OUR PARTS. WE WILL DO ANYTHING FOR OUR SONS.
MY PART WILL BE TO PLUNGE A BLADE INTO THE DOCTOR'S FLACCID FLESH. YOU WOULD BE WISE TO STAY BEHIND ME.

THEY
WAIT.

THEY ARE EXPECTING US. LET US SEE WHAT GIFTS THEY HAVE WROUGHT.

YES, LET US EMBRACE THE GLORY OF THE HUNT. LET THE SLOW RHYTHM OF THE DYING HEART AND THE SUDDEN SILENCE OF THE SCREAMING SOUL BE OUR TREASURE.

TONIGHT, THE BARRIER FALLS.

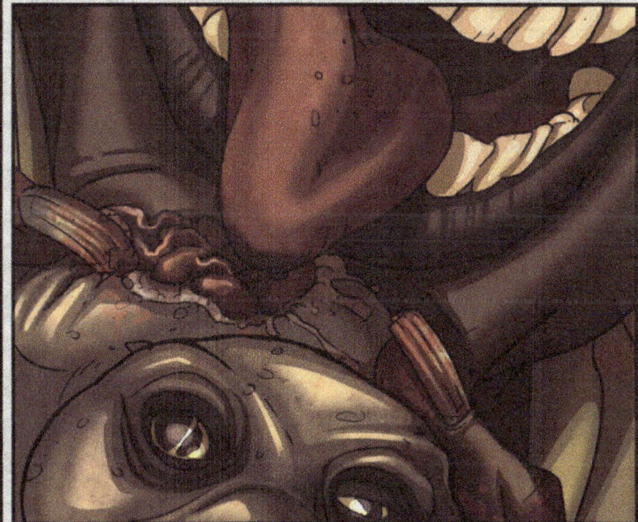

TONIGHT, WE SLAY GHOSTS!

THE NIGHT AWAITS.

BI, COMFORT THE LITTLE ONES. ROCK THEM AND LET SLEEP COME. THERE IS NOTHING THEY NEED TO SEE TONIGHT.

I WILL. HUSH NOW. THERE'S NOTHING TO FEAR.

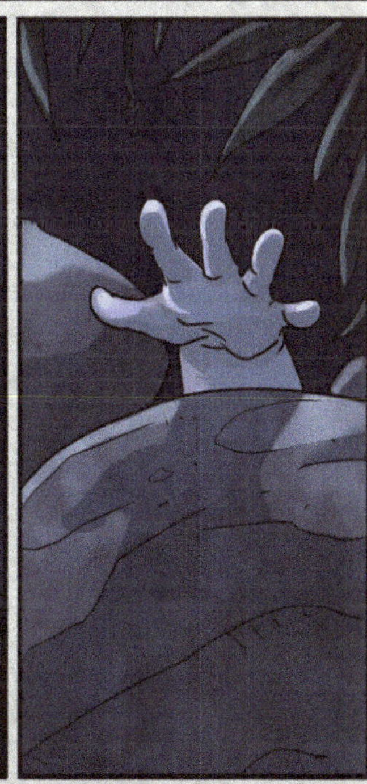

STAY WITH YOUR FRIENDS, LITTLE MAN. A DAY WILL COME WHEN YOU MUST FIGHT, BUT TODAY'S BATTLE IS MINE.
STAY.

I LOVE YOU, KWASI.

I LOVE YOU ALL.

HE'S COMING.

THE CREATURES OF THE NIGHT ARE QUIET.
THEY BOTH COME.

COME QUICKLY, REHEMA. TRUST IN SHAMIRA. SHE WILL PROTECT YOUR BOY.
I HAVE NO DOUBT.

AND FEAR?
SILENCED. LIKE THE NOCTURNAL BEASTS...

"THE SCENT OF DEATH TINGES THE AIR, AND THE WINDS CHANGE. THICKNESS CLINGS TO THE BACK OF MY THROAT - THE THICKNESS OF TAINTED BREATH. I'VE NEVER FELT ITS EQUAL, EVEN WHEN I CLAIMED IDI'S REMAINS...

"THE HARVESTER IS THE CORE OF MY VENGEFUL SPIRIT, BUT THE DOCTOR IS THE TRUE DANGER. HIDDEN AMONG A HUNDRED CHARLATANS, THE DOCTOR'S POWERS HAVE GROWN STRONG. I TASTE HIM LIKE A BILE IN THE AIR."
WE WILL FACE THE HARVESTER. WE WILL FACE THE NECROTIC BEASTS SUMMONED AT THE DOCTOR'S BEHEST.
YOU, REHEMA, GUIDED BY YOUR FATHER'S SPIRIT, MUST FACE THE DOCTOR. TASTE HIS EVIL, UNCOVER HIS SELF, AND THEN SPIT HIS CORPSE ONTO THE GROUND.
YOU ARE OUR GREATEST STRENGTH.

THE BARRIER FALLS.

OLD MAGICS...

WEAK MAGICS.

ONLY ONE HERE HAS TRUE STRENGTH.

POWERED BY THE BONDS OF LOVE, BUT LOVE... HMM... LOVE IS NOT THE ONLY POWER TYING A PARENT TO A CHILD...

FOR GUILT RUNS DEEP.

AGHHHHH!!!
THE SCREAMS OF THE GHOST!
THE SILENCE OF DEATH!
NOW, ALL YOUR POWER I CLAIM FOR MY MASTER. FOR MY SON... I AM THE HARVESTER!

UH!
AAAAAAAH!
WHERE IS THE GHOST I SEEK?

THERE... THE... THE GHOST... IS THERE.
BUT THERE IS ONLY ONE GHOST THAT I NEED.
THERE ARE MANY GHOSTS HERE.
MORE WILL JOIN YOU SOON.

THERE ARE TOO MANY!

HAH!

THE DOCTOR HAS NEITHER UNLIMITED RESOURCES NOR UNCEASING WILL.

WE NEED ONLY ALLOW REHEMA THE TIME TO DO AS SHE NEEDS.

I CAN'T... I CAN'T.

"YOU WILL. FOR THEM.

"FAMILY, BLOOD, LOVE.
"YOU WILL FIGHT. AND REHEMA...

THERE.
"SHE WILL FIND THE DOCTOR.

"AND SHE WILL END HIM."

PRETTY GHOST... PRETTY, PRETTY FLESH. RUN. FLEE. OR MY BLADE WILL TASTE OF THE WHITE.
NO.

NO? I SEE. IT IS OF NO CONSEQUENCE. YOU ARE NOTHING TO ME.

NOT EVEN A WOMAN.

THEN HARVEST! HARVEST MY BLOOD!

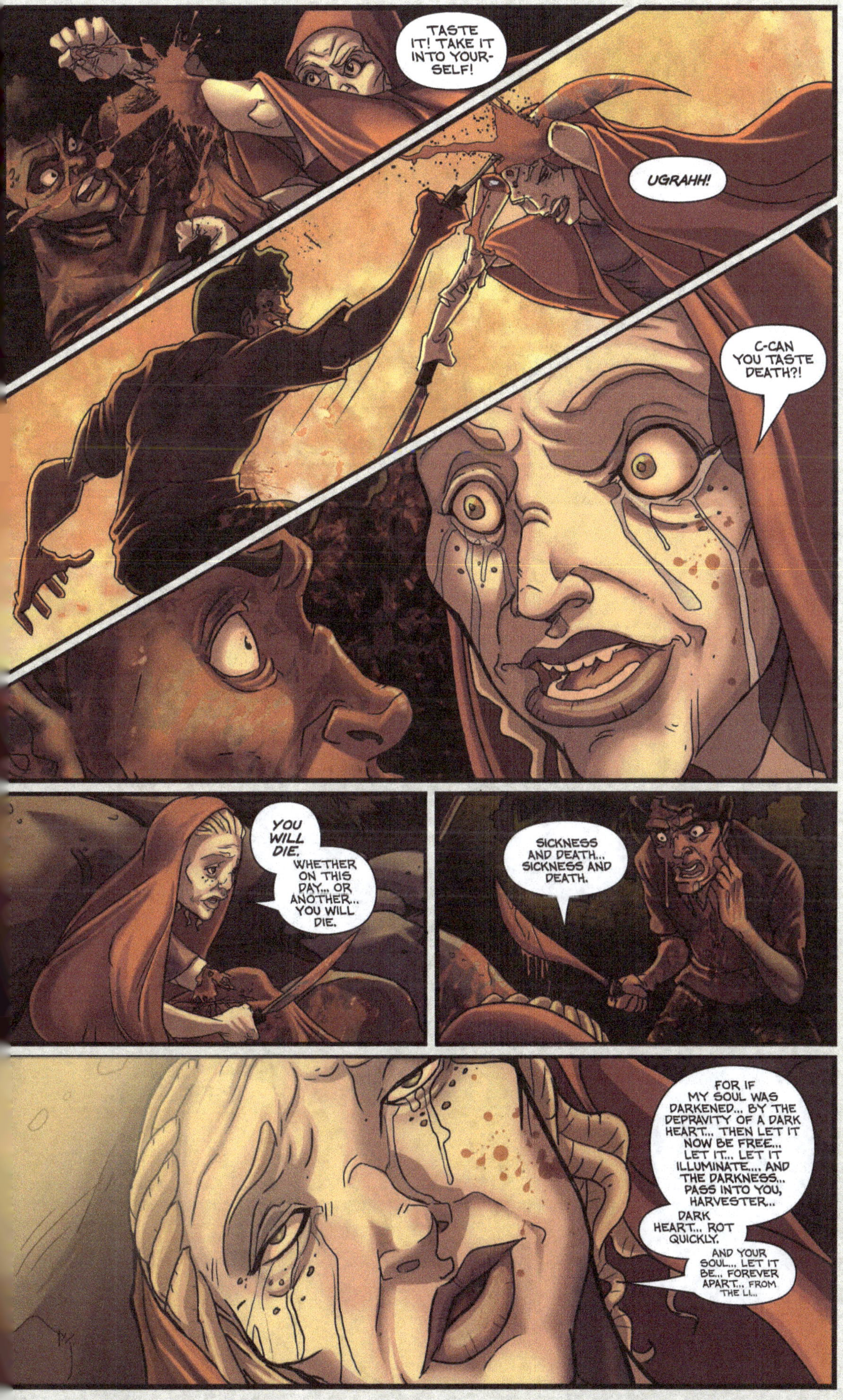

TASTE IT! TAKE IT INTO YOUR-SELF!
UGRAHH!
C-CAN YOU TASTE DEATH?!

YOU WILL DIE.
WHETHER ON THIS DAY... OR ANOTHER... YOU WILL DIE.

SICKNESS AND DEATH... SICKNESS AND DEATH.

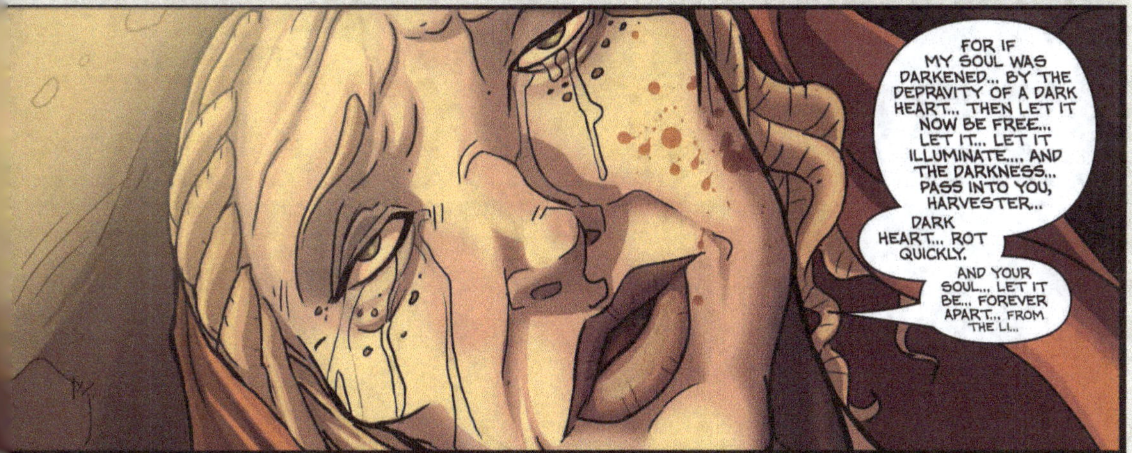

FOR IF MY SOUL WAS DARKENED... BY THE DEPRAVITY OF A DARK HEART... THEN LET IT NOW BE FREE... LET IT... LET IT ILLUMINATE.... AND THE DARKNESS... PASS INTO YOU, HARVESTER...
DARK HEART... ROT QUICKLY.
AND YOUR SOUL... LET IT BE... FOREVER APART... FROM THE LI...

AGGHHH!
SNIFF
YOU'RE A GHOST. A GHOST! NOT A WOMAN.
NO SICKNESS... NO SICKNESS.

EIGHT YEARS AGO
PLEASE, GOD, PROTECT HER.
"NOT A WOMAN...
ONE YEAR AGO
"NO SICKNESS...
"NO SICKNESS!"
SON!!!

HARVESTER!
WORTHLESS FOOL. YOU CANNOT BE A SLAVE TO YOUR PAST WHEN YOU BELONG TO ME.
REMEMBER THE FLESH. REMEMBER. REMEMBER.
HEAR THE BABE'S CRIES. GO TO HIM. CLAIM HIM. RECLAIM YOUR SON. REMEMBER THE FLESH!

YOU ARE NO ONE'S SAVIOR, DOCTOR.

MMMPH!

TIME NOW TO DRIFT TO THE GREAT BEYOND AND SEE WHAT YOUR FORTUNES HAVE WROUGHT.

FOR ALL PEACE CAN BE FOUND IN BREATH.

SUCH A QUIET END...

GET THE CHILDREN!

SOMEONE, GET THE CHILDREN!

QUICKLY!

WILLIAM! NO!

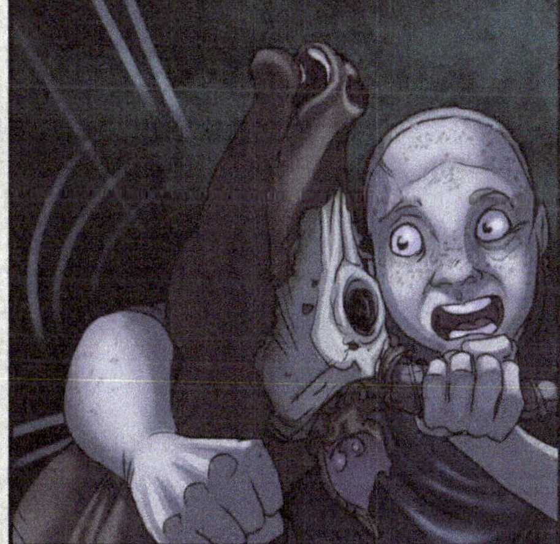

YOU MUST... GET THE YOUNG ONES! TAKE THEM AWAY FROM HERE. LET US FINISH.
LET US... FINISH...

STAY QUIET. YOU MUST STAY QUIET! WE CAN'T LEAVE YET. NOT UNTIL THEY COME FOR US.
IT'LL BE OVER SOON.
MAMA...

THEN... YOU MUST... LET HIM GO...
I CAN'T KEEP HIM DOWN!

NO!

JUST HOLD ON A BIT LONGER.
AGH!

CRK!

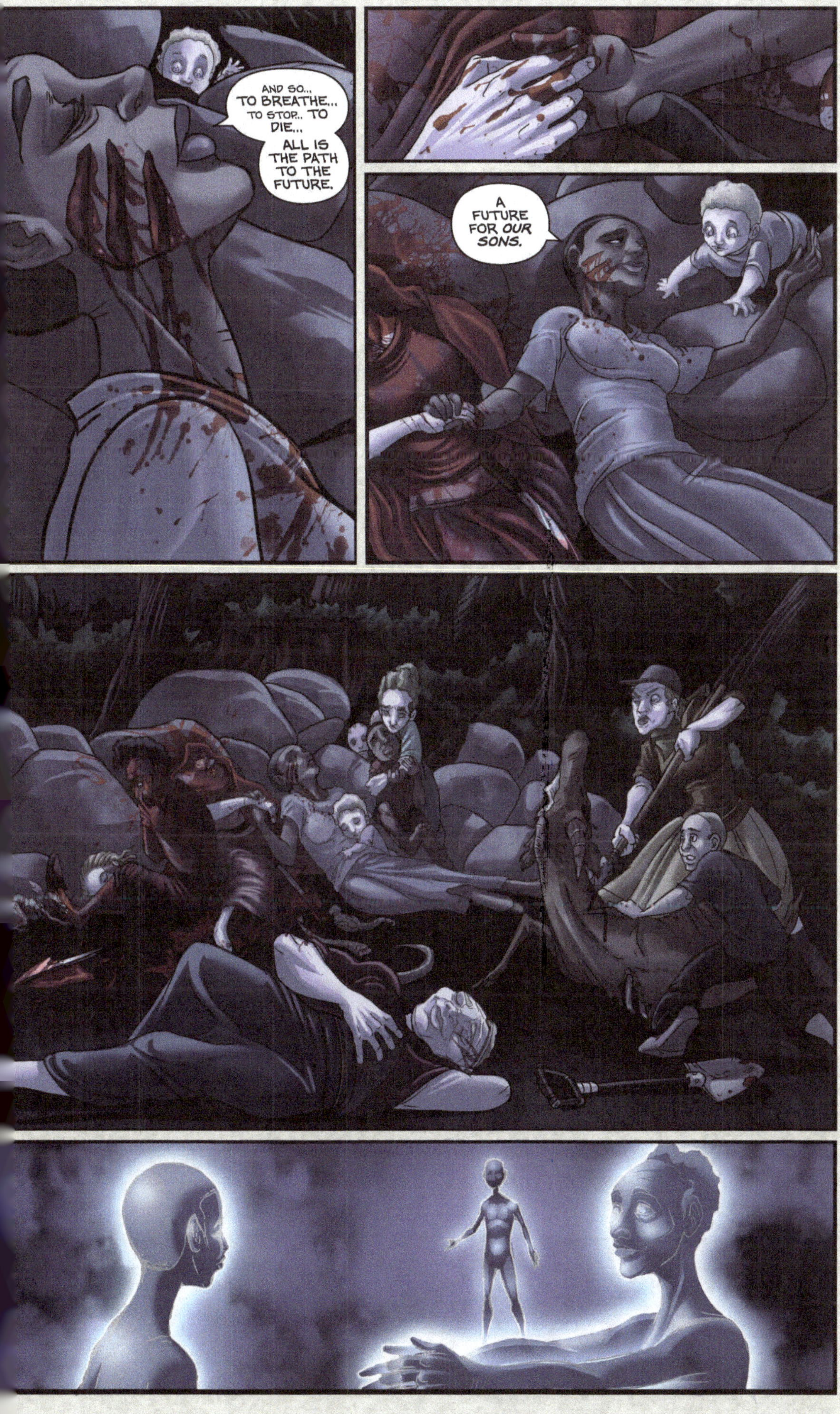

AND SO...
TO BREATHE...
TO STOP... TO DIE...
ALL IS THE PATH TO THE FUTURE.

A FUTURE FOR OUR SONS.

THE FUTURE

I AM TOO FAST FOR YOU, KWASI.

WAIT UP, MATHAYO!

WILLIAM SAYS I AM THE FASTEST AMONG US. PERHAPS ONE DAY I WILL EARN MY LIVING PLAYING FOOTBALL!
MAYBE FIRST YOU SHOULD LEARN TO SCORE A GOAL, EH?

YOU'RE READY?
YES...

IT'S A BEAUTIFUL DAY...
MAY THE BLESSINGS OF GENERATIONS PAST FIND YOU ON THIS DAY.

"MAY THE LOVE OF YOUR MOTHER AND FATHER SHINE UPON YOUR UNION--

"--AND YOUR LOVE BE AS STRONG AS THEIRS."

ARUSHA, TANZANIA

I WISH THEY'D STOP...
MAYBE WE SHOULDN'T BE HERE...

OF COURSE WE SHOULD. THERE'S A TIME TO HIDE, BUT THERE'S ALSO A TIME TO TEACH.
THAT TIME HAS COME.

"TO PROTECT WHAT I LOVE I WILL SHOW MY FACE. I WILL SHOW THAT I AM NOT TO BE FEARED. I AM NOT A GHOST.
"I AM A MAN."

A Ghost in the Grass

OR MAKE YOU LOOK THE FOOL.

BUT IF THERE WERE ANY FISH, I'M SURE YOU'VE SCARED THEM OFF BY NOW. LET'S GET OUT OF HERE.

AND DO WHAT?
FOOT-BALL?

DO YOU HEAR THAT?
SKTH
SKTH

YEAH. JUST KEEP YOUR HEAD DOWN. IT'LL BE FINE.

SKTH

SKTH

WHAT WAS THAT?
SHE... SHE JUST REMINDED ME OF MY MOTHER. THAT'S ALL.

SORRY, KWASI. JUST... BE CAREFUL. PEOPLE--

I KNOW. I KNOW. I HAVE MY PARENTS' STRENGTH, MATHAYO. MY FLESH DOESN'T DEFINE ME.

SKTH

COME ON, KWASI. WE SHOULD GO.

SHE COULD BE HURT.

SKKRREK!

I'LL BE RIGHT BACK.

WAIT UP!

SHHH.

MAMBA. IT WON'T RUN.
I KNOW.

GET THE WOMAN TO SAFETY.

THIS IS UNWISE.

I'LL KEEP MY DISTANCE. JUST MOVE HER AWAY WHEN THE SNAKE IS DISTRACTED.

READY?
READY.

HE'S... A GHOST.

NO. NOT YET.

WHY DOESN'T HE RUN?
MAMBA ARE TOO FAST AND NOT EASILY DECEIVED.
BETTER TO WAIT UNTIL THE MOMENT IS RIGHT.
NOW!

I HATE SNAKES.

ARE YOU OKAY?

YES, YES.
AND YOU? YOU'RE OKAY?

YES. IF YOU HADN'T...

WELL, THANK YOU.
BOTH OF YOU.

YOU MIGHT WANT TO WAIT A BIT BEFORE GRABBING YOUR STUFF... WE CAN WAIT WITH YOU, IF YOU'D LIKE.
YES, I THINK I'D LIKE THAT VERY MUCH.